INDIANA JONES™

AND THE
SARGASSO PIRATES
PART 4

STORY
KARL KESEL

PENCIL BREAKDOWNS
KARL KESEL & PAUL GUINAN

INKS & FINISHES
EDUARDO BARRETO

COLORS
BERNIE MIREAULT

LETTERS
PAT BROSSEAU

COVER ART
ALEX ROSS

Spotlight

DARK HORSE COMICS

VISIT US AT
www.abdopublishing.com

Reinforced library bound edition published in 2011 by Spotlight, a division of the ABDO Group, 8000 West 78th Street, Edina, Minnesota 55439. Spotlight produces high-quality reinforced library bound editions for schools and libraries. Published by agreement with Dark Horse Comics, Inc., and Lucasfilm Ltd.

Printed in the United States of America, Melrose Park, Illinois.
052010
092010
♻ This book contains at least 10% recycled materials.

Library of Congress Cataloging-in-Publication Data

Kesel, Karl.
  Indiana Jones and the Sargasso pirates / script [by] Karl Kesel ;
art [by] Eduardo Barreto.
     p. cm. -- (Indiana Jones and the Sargasso pirates ; 4)
  Summary: When Indiana Jones signs on with a band of pirates, he does not realize that his old nemesis is among them.
  ISBN 978-1-59961-761-9 (volume 1) -- ISBN 978-1-59961-762-6 (volume 2) -- ISBN 978-1-59961-763-3 (volume 3) -- ISBN 978-1-59961-764-0 (volume 4)
  1. Graphic novels. [1. Graphic novels. 2. Adventure and adventurers--Fiction. 3. Pirates--Fiction. 4. Sea stories.] I. Barreto, Eduardo, ill. II. Title.
  PZ7.7.K47 2011
  741.5'973--dc22
                                                                          2010006485

All Spotlight books have reinforced library bindings and
are manufactured in the United States of America.

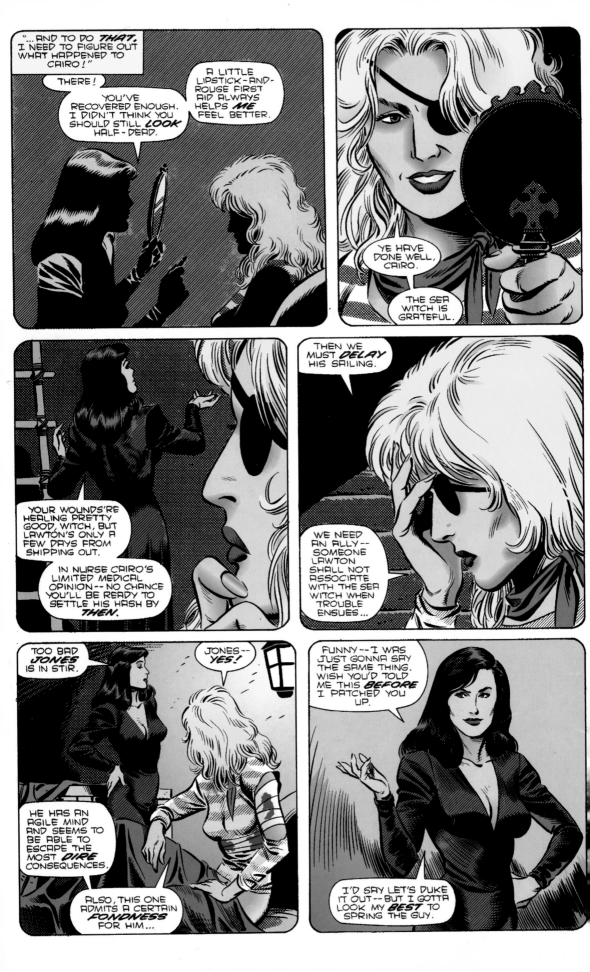

CAIRO!

HANG ON, WITCH! THIS IS GONNA BE A *ROUGH RIDE!*

I WILL *RETURN* FOR YE! THE SEA WITCH GIVES HER *WORD!*

GOTCHA, YOU TWO! C'MON -- A LITTLE FARTHER!

THERE!

YOU'RE *BLEEDING,* SEA WITCH.

A FEW SMALL WOUNDS REOPENED. THIS ONE WILL BE FINE.

AND IF SOME-ONE CUT OFF YOUR *ARM,* YOU'D SAY IT WAS A *BUG BITE.* LET ME LOOK...

EXPLOSION ROCKS SARGASSO!

SILENCE FOLLOWS DESPERATE GAMBIT! THIRTY MINUTES PASS... ONE HOUR...

SUDDENLY-- FROM THE OUTER EDGE OF THE SARGASSO'S MISTS...

LAWTON *DID* IT! HE GOT US OUT OF THE *SARGASSO!*

THAT PEG-LEGGED PIRANHA WAS FINALLY *GOOD* FOR SOMETHING!

KISS ME, JONES-- BEFORE I BUST!

THIS ONE... LIVED HER ENTIRE *LIFE* WITHIN THE FOG-SHROUDED SARGASSO...

SHE NEVER KNEW THE SKY ...THE *WORLD*... COULD BE SO *VAST*...

SEA WITCH-- GET *DOWN!* LAWTON'S MEN MIGHT *SEE* YOU!

THE INSTRUMENTS'RE *RESPONDIN'*, CAP'N, NOW WE'RE FREE A' THE *SARGASSO*...

DON'T *NEEDS* 'EM, MR. DRAKE. I KNOW THESE STARS BETTER'N THE SCARS A' ME OWN FACE.

TEN DEGREES PORT. STEADY AS SHE GOES.

A STIFF BREEZE AND SHIP FULL OF TREASURE AT OUR BACKS!

AH, YES-- A PIRATE'S LIFE FOR ME!

OF COURSE, I REGRET LEAVING *CAIRO* BEHIND. SHE HAD *MANY* TALENTS, BUT--

...*KILLS* ME... *JONES*...

...'R B'GOD... I'LL COMES BACK...

...*T'KILLS YOU*...

JONES!

BUDDA! BUDDA!

BUDA-BUDA

BUDA-BUDA

BUDDA! BUDDA! BUDDA!

CAIRO DISAPPEARS IN THE MUDDY WATER AND MAZE OF BOATS BEFORE THE BRITISH INSPECTOR CAN FIRE A SINGLE SHOT.

JOVE! THAT TOOK *COURAGE!*

AND SHE HAD IT TO *BURN!*

TRUE, A BRAVE LASS -- THE AUTHORITIES WILL HAVE TO BE NOTIFIED NEVERTHELESS.

THOUGH I SOMEHOW SUSPECT OUR MISS CAIRO WILL MAKE *GOOD* HER ESCAPE.

WHAT'RE THE CHARGES AGAINST HER, INSPECTOR?

BLACK-MARKETEERIN', FOR THE LARGE PART. A'COURSE, THERE ARE OTHER *RUMORS...*

I HEAR THE *NAZIS* WANT HER FOR STEALIN' STATE SECRETS!

TO BE TELLIN' THE TRUTH, DR. JONES, I DON'T KNOW WHICH SHE DESERVES MORE-- *PRISON* OR *PRAISE.*

I KNOW *EXACTLY* WHAT YOU MEAN.

DID YOU KNOW MISS CAIRO WAS TRAVELIN' WITH A RATHER *PORTLY* GENT WHO FANCIED HIMSELF YOUR *BROTHER?*

IMAGINE *THAT,* DR. JONES!

THE END